Francis Francis

The Angler's Register

SALZWASSER
VERLAG

Francis Francis

The Angler's Register

Reprint of the original, first published in 1859.

1st Edition 2022 | ISBN: 978-3-37513-160-9

Verlag (Publisher): Salzwasser Verlag GmbH, Zeilweg 44, 60439 Frankfurt, Deutschland
Vertretungsberechtigt (Authorized to represent): E. Roepke, Zeilweg 44, 60439 Frankfurt, Deutschland
Druck (Print): Books on Demand GmbH, In de Tarpen 42, 22848 Norderstedt, Deutschland

THE

ANGLER'S REGISTER,

𝔄 𝔏ist of the ℭome-at-able 𝔉isheries,

IN

ENGLAND, SCOTLAND, IRELAND AND WALES,

AND

HOW TO GET TO THEM, &c. &c. &c.

BY

FRANCIS FRANCIS.

LONDON:

TRÜBNER & CO., 60, PATERNOSTER ROW;

AND MAY BE HAD OF ALL FISHING. TACKLE MAKERS.

—

1858.

Price One Shilling.

PREFACE.

WHERE can I get comfortable quarters, pleasant scenery, and a little fishing? Where can I get a week or two's salmon fishing? Where shall we go for a day's fishing?—are questions which the compiler of the accompanying list has been asked, and has heard asked, very many times, without always being satisfactorily answered; and under the impression that such a list would be a boon to the angling world generally, and to all parties in any way connected with it, either directly or indirectly, he has been at considerable pains and labour in getting the materials together to form it. He has to thank many friends for their assistance and co-operation in this task, and many other persons to whom he has written for information for their prompt replies to his requests; he has also to express his acknowledgments to those who have forwarded additions or corrections since its original publication in the columns of THE FIELD. Owing to the short time there was to prepare the list, it is not so complete as the compiler could wish it to be; but, as it is his intention to publish an addendum next season, any communications will oblige, addressed to "F. F.," FIELD Office, Essex Street, Strand, London, W. C.

The introductory list of Scotch rivers was furnished by Andrew Young, Esq., well known for his long and consistent support to the salmon question in the columns of THE FIELD and various other papers; and as Scotland ranks first in the angling world, we place it at the commencement.

THE ANGLER'S REGISTER.

SCOTLAND.

RIVERS IN INVERNESS-SHIRE.

1. RIVER BEAULY.—In Lord Lovat's own hands.

2. RIVER NESS.—The lower part let to an angling club. The parts belonging to Lord Saltoun and Mr Bailey are to be let by the day; 6s. for one side of the river, or 10s. for both sides.

SUTHERLANDSHIRE, WEST COAST.

1. RIVER KIRKAIG.—Let to Mr T. Hutchinson, Bernard Castle.

2. RIVER INVER.—Let to Mr Mackenzie, Innkeeper, Lochinver, who lets it to anglers at 10s. 6d. a day.

8. RIVER LAXFORD.—Angling let, along with the deer forest of Stack, to Mr Dempster of Dunichen.

4. RIVER INSHARD, in the Duke of Sutherland's own hand.*

NORTH COAST.

5. RIVER GRUDY, in the Duke's own hand.

5. RIVER STRATHMORE.—Let with the deer forest to Lord Elcho.

7. RIVER HOPE, in the Duke's own hand.

8. RIVER BARGIE, in the Duke's own hand.

9. RIVER NAVER.—Let to Mr Ackroid.

10. RIVER STRATHY, in the Duke's own hand.

11. RIVER HALADALE, in the Duke's own hand.

EAST COAST.

12. RIVER HELMSDALE.—Let along with the grouse shooting to Mr. Hadwin and party.

13. RIVER BRORA.—Let to Mr Ackroid and party.

14. RIVER FLEET, in the Duke's own hand.

15. RIVER SHIN.—Let to Mr Young of Invershin, who lets it to anglers by the month, the rods never to exceed four; June and August of this year still unlet. [This is the river so often cited as the scene of a great feat of "Ephemera:" here he took some almost fabulous amount

---

* The rivers in the Duke's own hand are mostly small, with plenty of fish in them when there *is* water, and they usually go with the shootings.

of salmon, in a very short time—something like forty, I think it was, in two days.—*Author's note.*]

16. RIVER CASSLEY.—In the hands of the proprietor, Sir Charles Ross, of Balnagown.

17. RIVER OYKEL.—Let to Mr Robertson and party along with Strathoykel grouse shootings.

CAITHNESS-SHIRE.

The principal river in this county (Thurso), is let to Mr Dunbar of Brawl Castle, who sublets it to anglers.

ROSS-SHIRE.

1. RIVER CARRON.—Belongs to several proprietors. The part belonging to Sir Charles Ross lets by the day: apply to Mr Kingham, Ardgay, Bonar Bridge.

2. RIVER CONAN.—In the hands of several proprietors, all of whom at times grant permission.

———

THE THURSO (Salmon and Trout), Caithness.—Good from February to the middle of May, but not a summer river. Route: by rail to Aberdeen, and thence by steamer to Wick, and on by chaise sixteen miles to Thurso. Excellent accommodation at Brawl Castle. No cruives on the river. Restricted to seven rods, at 80*l.* per season, and 50*s.* per week board. Monthly tickets at from 15*l.* to 25*l.* per month are sometimes to be had. One fish per day allowed. A very easy river to fish, and sport seldom fails, even when the river is at the lowest; indeed, we have known ten or eleven fish killed to a rod when the river was dead low.* Fish of good size, from six pounds to twenty-five; few grilse. Flies to be obtained on the spot of Mr Dunbar. Excellent coast shooting at wild fowl, and good brown trout fishing in Loch Watten and other lochs in the neighbourhood; very few sea trout. Should the angler desire to see the country, and prefer coach to steamer, he can travel by coach *viâ* Inverness; but, although the scenery is very fine and varied, the journey is tedious. Address W. Dunbar, Esq., Brawl Castle, Thurso, Caithness, N.B.

THE INVER AND KIRKAIG† (Salmon and Trout).—Good summer rivers. Route: rail to Aberdeen, and on by coach to Loch Inver; or, rail to Glasgow, and thence by steamer to Loch Inver. Excellent accommodation at the inn, 2*l.* 5*s.* per week; servants 25*s.* Terms for salmon and sea trout fishing, the latter of which is very good, 10*s.* 6*d.* a

---

* Sixteen have been killed in one day this season by one rod.
† Both of these rivers have been since let.

day, or 12*l.* a month. Four rods on the Inver, two on the Kirkaig. No charge made for brown trout fishing. There are forty lochs containing brown trout, and on some of them are boats for the purpose of trolling for Salmo ferox, &c. Address to Thos. M'Kenzie, Loch Inver Inn, by Lairg.

THE NESS (Salmon).—By joining the club at Inverness, subscription 2*l.* 2*s.* Accommodation close to the river in the Union or Caledonian hotels. Middle of July to the end of August the best season. Flies at Inverness. The fish are chiefly grilse, but a few salmon may be got; or see Lord Saltoun's and Mr Bailey's portions, per Mr Young's list.

THE SPREY, on a portion of it, leave may sometimes be obtained at Fochabers, from the Duke of Richmond's factor there. All fish have to be given up. Rail to Aberdeen, thence by coach.

THE UGIE, near Peterhead, a few salmon and plenty of sea trout. This water is rented by a club. Rail to Aberdeen. The Y-than, twelve miles from Aberdeen, at Newburgh is open. There is good trout fishing, and at times plenty of sea trout.

THE DON, at Aberdeen. In the tideway, good sea trout fishing may be had, and it is not difficult to obtain leave below the cruives. At Alford bridge, about twenty-seven miles up, Mr. Feniman, the innkeeper, reserves a right of fishing for his customers. Flies at Mr. Brown's, tackle maker, Aberdeen, for the rivers about Aberdeen.

LOCHARD (Trout and Pike), Aberfoyle, Perthshire.—At Blair's Hotel. Rail from Stirling or Balloch to Buchlyvie, thence seven miles by gig to Aberfoyle. Trout fishing very good. Average weight, half-a-pound each, lively on the hook, and cutting up red. Flies. 1. Wing, white tip from wing of mallard, red body, black hackle, gold tinsel. 2. Teal drake wing, red, yellow or green body, red hackle, gold tinsel. 3. Grouse wing, hare's ear body, ginger hackle. 4. Raven's wing, black body, black hackle, &c. The trout take a spinning minnow freely. The sport here this April and May has been much above the same months of former years. April and May are the best for the fly. There are also pike of great size. Charge, 5*s.* 6*d.* per day for boat and man, who supplies minnows. The scenery on this lake is unsurpassed.

LOCH KATTERINE, Trossachs.—McGregor's Hotel, or McIntyre's Hotel, Bridge of Turk, twenty-six miles from Stirling, coaches every day during summer. The trout fishing here is very good; they run from one-third of a lb. up to two and three lbs. weight; they take to the minnow and fly freely; flies, nearly the same as those used on Lochard, but larger. The fish are very fine yellow fellows, red in the flesh, and well flavoured. June and July are the best months. Boats rather expensive, to be had by applying at McGregor's Hotel.

LOCHS ACHRAY AND VENNACHER communicate with Loch Katterine. The trout in these lakes grow to a large size. They do not rise well at the fly in Loch Vennacher, preferring the minnow. Salmon frequent both these lakes. Large pike are often taken. Boats to be had, for Loch Vennacher, by applying at McGregor's Hotel, Callander, or McIntyre's Hotel, Bridge of Turk; and for Loch Achray, from McGregor's Hotel, Trossachs. About two miles south of Achray is Drunkie, an excellent Loch, containing abundance of fine bright Trout. The scenery of the Trossachs, so well described in the Lady of the Lake, needs no comment.

THE TUMMEL (Salmon and Trout).—About a mile may be fished by staying at the hotel (Mr Fisher's) at Pitlochrie; best time towards the end of May according to season. Route: rail to Perth, coach to Pitlochrie. Fishing fair. The angler, if lucky, *may* get his fish a day.

LOCH ERICHT we understand may be fished by stopping at the inn at Dalwhinnie. The trout average half a lb. Rail to Perth. Thence *viâ* Blair Athol.

LOCH RANNOCH (Good Trout fishing).—By stopping at the inn at Tighnalin, and making application to Struan Robertson and Lady Menzies. From Perth by coach *viâ* Aberfeldie.

THE TAY (Salmon and Trout).—By staying at the Birnan Hotel, Dunkeld, near Perth, a small portion of the Tay can be fished. Flies, &c. for the last three places, Paton and Walsh, Perth; or by sending an order to Martin, Glasgow, or Lang, Hanover-street, Edinburgh.

LOCH AWE (Trout).—By staying at the inn at Dalmally. Rail to Glasgow, and steamer *viâ* Loch Lomond. Good trolling for the Salmo ferox and other trout.

ST. MARY'S LOCH AND THE YARROW (Trout), Selkirkshire.—By stopping at Tibby Shiels's. Good stream and burn fishing also in the neighbourhood; but pike have increased of late years in the loch, where the trout fishing is hardly so good as formerly in consequence. For flies to suit send to Lang's, Hanover-street, Edinburgh. Engage a room a week beforehand, by writing to Mrs Richardson, St. Mary's, Yarrow, Selkirkshire. Route: rail *viâ* Carlisle, to Moffat, thence fifteen miles by gig to Yarrow. Pleasant scenery, and comfortable but homely quarters. Good perch fishing on the adjoining loch (the loch of the Lowes).—N.B. The angler must take all wines and spirits with him, as the house is not licensed. From here the angler can cut across to the Crook inn below Tweedsmuir, where, if the season be favourable, he will get good *trout* fishing in the Tweed and several smaller streams in the neighbourhood.

LOCH LEVEN (Trout), Kinross.—Rail *viâ* Stirling, within a short distance of Kinross. The tacksman, Mr Marshall, supplies a boat and two men at 2*s*. 6*d*. an hour; and if the angler be fortunate he may secure an overflowing creel of very beautiful trout, on a fine sheet of water with the old castle and its historical associations to repose in (if he chooses) during the heat of the day.

ABERFELDY (Salmon and Trout).—Fishing on a portion of the river Lyon and other rivers, with good loch fishing, can he had by stopping at the Breadalbane Arms, with occasional permission on other good preserved waters. Fine scenery and good accommodation. Route: Perth by rail, Aberfeldy by coach. The river fishing is good till the end of May, when the loch fishing begins. Flies at Paton and Walsh's, Perth. Further particulars may be had by applying to W. P. Mackenzie, Breadalbane Arms and Caledonian Hotels, Aberfeldy, near Perth.

LOCH EILT AND THE RIVER AYLORT (Salmon and Trout), thirty miles from Fort William.—Accommodation at Kinloch and Aylort Inn, which is two miles from the loch. Terms, one rod, with boat and man, 1*l*. per day, or 4*l*. per week; two rods, with boat and man to row, 1*l*. 10*s*. per day, or 6*l*. per week. The angler to keep his own fish. No cross-lines or other fishing allowed. The tenter, Angus Macdonald, who lives at the lake, gives all the necessary assistance to fishermen; and Mr Gunning, Rhue, Arasaig, *viâ* Fort William, will answer all letters and inquiries. Route: To Glasgow by rail, and on to Oban by steamer, *viâ* Lochgilphead and the Crinan Canal. From Oban to Fort William, either by coach road, which is the shortest, or by Dalmally and Glencoe, and on to Arasaig. The angler or tourist will be well repaid for the length of his journey, by the fine scenery and the historical recollections it calls up.

IRELAND.

[Previous to fishing for Salmon in Ireland, the angler must take out a certificate.]

THE GALWAY RIVER (Salmon and Sea Trout.)—Route: By rail to Holyhead, thence by steamer to Dublin, and on by rail to Galway. Messrs. Ashworth are the proprietors of the river. The lessee is Mr. Andrew Buist. The river is open to visitors to Galway on application to Mr. Buist's manager, Mr. Miller, who is very civil and obliging. One salmon a day (the best) is allowed. The river is short, and a good deal fished by the people in the town; but the angler will see large numbers of salmon, and, if he is there at the right time, he will hardly fail to have good sport. Lawless the tackle maker in the town, supplies good and cheap flies for the river, and also for all the Connemara lakes and rivers. There are several hotels. Early and late in the season are the best times, June and the early part of July being of little use. A shrimp is a very favourite bait with the salmon here, and the sea trout and salmon also take worms and spinning baits better than in most rivers.

LOUGH CORRIB, from which the Galway river runs, holds very large pike, Salmo ferox, besides salmon and brown trout. Pike of large size are also very numerous, but are chiefly taken by "spillets," set at night. Pat Hickey, of the Wood Quay, Galway, is the best and most civil attendant in Lough Corrib. Oughterard, about twelve or fifteen miles from Galway, would be the best station for the angler to fish it from. It is open to all. There is a nice little trout stream at Oughterard, and between there and Clifden are a considerable number of lakes, which require little leave to fish, or may be fished by stopping at any of the little wayside houses.

BALLINAHINCH.—Further on towards Clifden is the well-known, far-famed Salmon and Trout Fishing of Ballinahinch.—To fish Ballina-hinch fishery, the angler must take the Bianconi stage car, which runs through Oughterard to Clifden, and which will drop him at a little inn called The Recess; or he may go on by car from Recess to Roundstone, whichever the angler prefers to stop at. Recess is nearest the lakes; Roundstone to the river. It is a summer fishery principally, but contains a few salmon in the spring. The lake fishing for sea trout about July and August is excellent; but the salmon fishing is indifferent, the weir being kept so close. Flies to be had of Lawless, Galway. Terms: 5s. per day, exclusive of boats, if fishing on the lakes. There are several very good lakes, and the river; seal shooting at Roundstone. Accommodation tolerable at the inns at Recess and Roundstone.

THE DOOHALLA FISHERY (Trout).—Mr Young's lakes, about three or four miles from Roundstone, or five or six from Clifden; 5s. per day, 1s. to each boatman. The best white trout fishing in Connemara, and perhaps in Ireland. The fish run large, and are very plentiful in July and August. Salmon are being introduced into the lakes, but, as yet, are not allowed to be killed. The angler can find accommodation either at Roundstone or Clifden. Between these places are numerous brown trout lakes, where the angler can fish without question; and nearer Clifden is a small lake (Ballinahoy), containing a few salmon and white trout, which can be fished by stopping at the inn at Clifden. It is hardly worth notice, however.

KYLEMORE (Salmon and Trout.)—Fairish fishing to be had here

by stopping at the inn some seven miles from Clifden. The scenery is also fine.

THE BLACKWATER (Salmon and Trout), Cork.—Either by rail from Dublin, or by steamer from Bristol to Cork, thence to Lismore. Very fair fishing to be obtained by application to Messrs Cliffe and Foley, the lessees. All fish given up. Flies to be obtained from Hackett, tackle-maker, Cork, or the fisherman (Ray). March and April or June and July (when the grilse are running) are the best months. The angler may obtain leave to fish almost any part of the Blackwater by writing a polite note to the owners of the various waters; but he will always have to give up the fish. Good lodgings at Lismore, at Mrs O'Brien's.

THE LEE (Salmon and Trout).—By ticket, 2s. 6d. a day or 12s. per week. Route to Cork as above. Apply to Mr Hackett, 38, Partridge-street, Cork. The fishing is very good. There is a mile and a half of water, alternate pool and stream. The angler is permitted to keep his fish. Hackett will supply flies, tickets, &c.

THE KERRY BLACKWATER (Salmon and Trout).—Leave obtained of Mr Mahony, Dromore Castle, or by stopping at the Blackwater Hotel, J. M'Clure, Old Dromore, about ten miles from Killarney and seven from Kenmare. The Roughty can also be fished, but is so much poached as to be hardly worth while. Killgarven (seven miles from Kenmare) would be the best station for it. Route : rail or packet to Cork, Killarney, and thence by car. Flies, Flint of Dublin, or Hackett of Cork.

WATERVILLE (Salmon and Trout), Kerry.—Leave by stopping at the hotels. Good fishing and fine scenery, sea bathing, &c. March and April is the best for salmon, and from June onward for the white trout, which are plentiful and large. Route viâ Killarney. Flies, &c. to be had at Waterville, or as before.

LOCH MELVIN (Salmon and Trout), Garrison, Fermanagh.—By stopping at Scott's Inn, or the Bailiff's on the loch. Very good salmon fishing until the middle of May. In June grilse come in, and show fair sport. Excellent trout fishing of various sorts. Many fine gillaroo trout may be caught. Boat and two men, 4s. a day. Board, 2l. 2s. per week. Flies at the tackle-maker's, at Ballyshannon.—N.B. To fish the best parts of this loch it would be advisable to apply to Mr Johnstone, of Kinlough House, Loch Melvin, who seldom refuses. The Bundrowse river runs out of the lake ; and to fish it the angler must stop at Bundoran, a pleasant little watering place. Route : rail to Enniskillen, and thence by coach.

THE ERNE (Salmon and Trout), Ballyshannon, Donegal, a few miles from Loch Melvin.—Leave of the proprietor, Dr. Shiel. The angler will find it uncertain about obtaining leave, not from any disinclination to grant it upon the part of the proprietor, but in consequence of large numbers of applications. The river would carry about ten rods, and there are often twenty old friends and acquaintances of the owner waiting their turn. But if the angler likes good trout-fishing, he will find by going to the little inn at Belleek and fishing Loch Erne the finest trout in the world, delicious in flavour, and running from about two to twenty pounds' weight. The loch, too, abounds in pike, perch, and bream, of which last fish cartloads might be taken in some spots. The angler will find little difficulty in getting permission here. Route, flies, &c., &c. as before.

LOUGH ESKE (Trout and Char), Donegal.—A beautiful loch, containing large trout, and an abundance of char, and in the season a tolerable supply of sea trout and a few salmon. The char do not take well until the middle of July, when good sport may be had with them. The right of fishing belongs to T. Brooke, Esq., of Lough Eske House, Straban, who will readily grant leave and the use of his boat to *gentlemen* upon application. Inquire about flies, &c., at the hotel at Donegal. Route by mail car from Ballyshannon.

THE OWENEA (Salmon and Trout), Ardara, Donegal.—This river belongs to W. Tredennick, Esq., Fort William, Ballyshannon, and good sport may at times be had upon it, if the angler is so fortunate as to be upon the spot at the time of a spate; but, as it rises and falls very quickly, it would be hardly worth his while to go there upon the chance. There are, however, in the neighbourhood, some good brown-trout lochs which are open, where the trout, though ugly and black, run of good size. The route would be by mail car from Donegal to Killybegs, and thence by car to Ardara, or by car from Donegal to Ardara or Glenties.

THE GWEEBARRA (Salmon and Trout), Donegal, belongs to Mr Daniel, of Donegal. The same may be said of this river as the last. The angler or tourist will have to take car from Glenties and Dungloe, some six or seven miles further on, as the best practicable stopping place between the Gweebarra and Dungloe; and further on to Gweedore there are an immense number of small lochs, all open, some of which contain very fine and handsome yellow trout five or six pounds weight. Others contain myriads of small trout (about six to the pound), any number of which may be taken in a day. At Dungloe, if the angler choses to diversify his proceedings, he may get excellent seal and wild fowl shooting. At Gweedore there is a capital hotel, a perfect oasis in the desert, built by Lord G. Hill, for the accommodation of tourists—clean, good attendance, a fair supply of edibles and potables, and very reasonable. There are here two small rivers and two very good small trout lochs, which, later in the season, hold sea trout and some few salmon. Should the angler be here during a spate, he may chance to get his three or four salmon a day in the river. There is nothing to pay for fishing, and only 1s. each to the men who row the boat when he goes upon the lakes for small brown trout, of which there is great abundance. (The author took sixteen dozen each day on two successive days, in hot sultry weather. Had the days been favourable the take might easily have been doubled. The sixteen dozen weighed about thirty-five pounds.) Almost any flies will do; something with red or black hackle, and a mixture with hare's ear in it.

The Lennan and Loch Fern (Salmon and Trout), Rathmelton, Donegal.—This excellent loch and river belong to Jas. Watt, Esq., of Claraugh, Rathmelton. On anything like a good day, one, two, or three salmon may be taken on the loch, and numbers of fine brown trout. The principal difficulty the angler will experience will be in getting a boat. There are but two on the loch, one of which is a joint-stock affair belonging to five or six gentlemen, and the other is private. It is needless to say that when the weather is favourable the owners are most probably using them; still the landlord of the inn might probably be able to get over the difficulty. There is a sweep in the town who ties a tolerable fly. The trout fishing on the river is rather good; and if the river be in good order, the angler may seduce a few white trout, or a salmon or two, out of one of the lower pools—particularly if he can get leave to fish the mill pool, which is *not* included in the general permit. It is a very early river. The *best* way to Rathmelton is *viâ* Derry—which is reached by rail.

The Bann and The Bush are rivers which were good, but, from a variety of causes, are now indifferent. There is good trout fishing in the former, but it is much fished. All we know of the latter is that it has been constantly in the market, and apparently but seldom found a bidder for it.

The Moy (Salmon and Trout), Ballina.—From Dublin by rail to Enniskillen, thence by Bianconi car, *viâ* Sligo, to Ballina. Open to visitors upon application to Mr Little, the weir-owner. Boat and attendance, 5s. per day. All fish returned at the weir, or taken at the market price. The fish in the Moy are small but plentiful, being mostly grilse, with an occasional salmon. Accommodation at the hotels middling. If the angler likes boat fishing, and is fortunate, he may kill five or six fish or more a day here. As many as twenty have been killed. For flies, boats, &c., Pat Hearns, of Mill-street, will supply all that is needful. A few miles from Ballina is Loch Conn, a large loch, where there are a few very large trout and pike, and fine perch; sport, however, is rather uncertain, unless the angler doesn't mind spinning for perch, and considering that sport.

THE OWENMORE (Salmon and Trout).—From Ballina the angler can get to Bangor, by mail car; and, by stopping at the inn there, he will get leave to fish this *nice-looking river*. After the heavy floods of spring and autumn good sport may be had; but at other times it is indifferent, as the weir has no gap in it, and the mouth is rather closely fished. There is a large loch, and two other small rivers near it.

THE OWENDUFF (Salmon and Trout).—A very pretty river indeed to fish, and preserved principally for angling (no cruives), is about five miles from Bangor. The upper and best portion of it, about twelve miles, may be fished by taking a monthly ticket—the charge being 70*l.* per season, or about 25*l.* per month. This includes lodging and attendance; but it would not cost the angler more than about 2*s.* a day to board himself there. The fish are heavy and abundant, and the sea trout fishing excellent. The accommodation is at the lodge at Lacduff. Apply for further information to Mr Farlow, fishing·tackle maker, 191, Strand. The flies for these last two rivers are peculiar. Pat Hearns, of Ballina, might supply them; and there is a travelling fly-tier who sometimes comes to Bangor with flies. This river is the far-famed Ballycroy spoken of by Maxwell in his " Wild Sports of the West."

AT NEWPORT, co. Mayo, there is a river belonging to Mr Sidney Herbert, at the head of which is a very good loch, Loch Beltra. By staying at the inn at Newport, leave for one rod can be obtained. Further than this leave must be obtained of Mr Herbert's agent, for whose address (he does not live at Newport, but at Dublin) the angler, if he purposes to go to Newport, had better previously write to Mrs Bird, the landlady of the hotel at Newport. The angler, if on the river at the right time, may have good sport both with salmon and sea trout; but it gets so over-thrashed that they soon get shy. The river is by no means a nice one to fish, being more like a dyke than a river. The difficulty of the fishing at Loch Beltra lies in getting the boat, without which the fishing is useless; but should the angler obtain the boat, he will have capital sport there. There are other good lochs in the neighbourhood, to all of which Mrs Bird has the *entrée*. There will be little difficulty in finding out the flies at Newport, as there are plenty of fishermen. The best route to Newport is to Galway by rail; thence by mail, *viâ* Ballinrobe, to Westport. Newport Bay, with its numerous islands, is very fine; and the sail to Achill Head beautiful, and deservedly admired. At Achill the cliffs are stupendous, being some 1800 feet in height.

THE COSTELLO (Salmon and Trout), Galway.—This excellent river is fished by a club, and affords first-rate sport; but it is difficult to get into the club, memberships being in great request.

SOUTH WALES.

THE USK (Salmon and Trout), Abergavenny.—By season, 2l. 2s.; per day, for salmon 3s. 6d., trout 2s.; per week, 10s. salmon, 5s. trout. To be had of Mr Batt, or at the Angel Hotel. Route: Great Western to Hereford. Near here also is an excellent stream, the Monnow, and a fine brook the Onde, with another good brook the Grina. Leave is not difficult to obtain, but the brooks want water.

THE USK AND WYE (Salmon and Trout), Brecon.—Mr. T. Cummins, Castle Hotel. By staying here the angler can fish a large extent of well-preserved water. The terms for board, &c., with the right of fishing, are 2l. 2s. per week. Great Western Railway to Hereford, on by railway to Abergavenny, and thence to Brecon by coach at four p.m. Not far from Brecon is a famous pool for pike and perch, Llanors Pool. It is open.

THE WYE (Salmon and Trout) Builth, with smaller trout streams, &c.—Welfield Arms and Lion Hotels. Mr John Davies gives permission to visitors over four miles, preserved; board moderate. Route: Great Western Railway, and by rail viâ Hereford and Leominster to Kington, on by coach.

THE WYE (Salmon and Trout), and several smaller streams and lakes, Morgan's Hotel, Rhayader, Radnor. Mr. D. Morgan gives permission to visitors. A large extent of waters fishable. Route as before.

THE TOWY AND CORTHY (Trout), Carmarthen.—Fishable by day-ticket, price 1s. 6d., obtained at Carmarthen. Route: Great Western and South Wales railways. The Trout in the Towy are of good size—or rather, we should say, used to be, as we have been informed that the river is not now worth the angler's notice, being netted from end to end by poachers.

NORTH WALES.

THE DOVEY (Salmon and Trout), Machynlleth, Montgomeryshire.—For tickets, or permission, the angler will apply to Mr C. J. Lloyd, Wynnstay Arms Hotel. The fishing is very fair here, and the netting more restrained than formerly. Route: North Western Railway to Shrewsbury, and on by rail.

The Dovey (Salmon and Trout), Mallwyd, Montgomery.—Permission by staying at the Peniarth Arms, Mr Rowland's. Lake fishing in the neighbourhood. North Wales Railway to Oswestry, whence the coach goes *viá* Mallwyd, *on Monday, Wednesday, and Friday* only.

Ogwen Lake (Trout), near Bangor, Carnarvon.—By stopping at the inn at Capel Currig, or Douglas Arms at Bethesda, Mr Hughes's, boats can be obtained. The sport is good here, and the trout average half a pound. The scenery also is fine. There are two or three other good lakes in the neighbourhood. Route: North-Western and Chester and Holyhead lines to Bangor.

Carnarvon (Salmon and Trout).—There are three rivers here—the Sciont, the Giynphaw, and the Lyfni, which are all open, and where the fishing is tolerable from 1st of February to May, and from August to the end of October; but the salmon are not very plentiful. There are also several lakes in the neighbourhood. The Castle hotel will be found reasonable, and there are lodgings to be had in the town at all rates. Route as before.

River and Lake (Trout and Salmon), at Bedgellert, thirteen miles from Carnarvon. Prince Llewellyn Inn, or lodgings. Route as before, and on by coach.

Capital Lake Fishing over about ten lakes, and river fishing communicating therewith. Board and lodging, private, 8*l.* 3*s.* per week. Apply to Mr Hamer, Segontium-terrace, Carnarvon, who will supply the angler with all necessary information with regard to the various lakes and rivers in North Wales, and who arranges and superintends tours, with board, &c.

Coron Lake, Anglesea (Trout).—Bodorgan Arms; reasonable terms; trout fine (for Wales). Bodorgan railway station, on Chester and Holyhead line. Meilog Lake and the rivers of the two lakes are also fishable.

The Conway.—There is also good salmon and trout fishing to be obtained on the Conway; but we have no information about it. Doubtless, the angler going to any of the above neighbourhoods would easily supply the deficiency. There is good fishing also on parts of the Dee; and the angler desirous of fine scenery may enjoy it by going to the lovely vale of Llangollen, *viá* North-Western, and Shrewsbury and Oswestry Railway, to the King's Head Royal Hotel.

ENGLAND.

The Lake District (Trout).—The Greta and Derwent (preserved), by season ticket, price 5*s.*, taken of the Angling Association at Keswick.

Good accommodation at Keswick ; lovely scenery and fair sport. Rail to Penrith ; coach to Keswick. Wastwater, *via* Whitehaven Railway, to Drigg station.

At WAST WATER there is a good Inn ; fish plentiful, but moderate in quality, some very large ones may be taken with the minnow, but are seldom caught above half a pound with the fly. Burnmoor Tarn is about three miles from the head of the Lake. Trout there are of a good size and splendid eating. Large pike in it also. About the best lake for sport with fly of any in Cumberland is Crummock Tarn, but fish only moderate eating. Not very far from Wast Water is a small Lake belonging to Mr. Stanley, called Dovock Water. The fish there are excellent, but the sport is uncertain. Any one may angle fairly on it, and have the use of the boat. There are some quiet countrified Inns about three miles from it, and the scenery is very grand.

At Nether Wastdale there is a comfortable inn. The lake is free. At Penrith, on the Lancaster and Carlisle line, he can fish the Eamont, and Ullswater from Appleby or Brough.

THE ULLSWATER fishing is moderate ; the hotel at Patterdale first rate. A mile and a half from Patterdale is Angle Tarn, where, on any favourable day, a man may catch a creel full of superb trout as to quality, but not very large.

A few miles from either Penrith or Shap station, on the same line, he can fish the Eden. The trout in the Lake District generally are not large ; and only those in Burnmoor Tarn and Dovoch Water are *really* worth eating. The angler will find much useful information on the Lake District in Dr. Davy's chatty little book "The Angler in the Lake District," to be had at all tackle makers.

THE LUNE (Trout), Kirkby Lonsdale.—*Via* Great Northern line to Leeds, on to Hornby on the Little North-Western line. There is an association forming here to protect the river. Dawson's Royal Hotel or the Green Dragon will be found both comfortable and moderate. Healthy, and fine scenery.

THE WENNING (Trout), Yorkshire.—Rail, *via* Leeds, to the Clapham station on the North-Western Railway. Stop at the Horseshoe Inn, close to the station. There are numerous streams in the neighbourhood, in which the landlord gives leave.

THE WHARFE (Trout and Grayling), Yorkshire.—Rail, *via* Leeds, to Skipton station on the North-Western Railway. Thence by fly to Bolton five miles. An excellent Inn at Bolton Bridge, and the trout fishing very good in the grounds of the Duke of Devonshire, at Bolton Abbey. Free to persons living at the Inn. Also from Skipton by fly to Kilnsey ten miles; there is excellent trout fishing in the water preserved by the Kilnsey Angling Association, subscription 3*l.* per annum. Strangers 2*s.* 6*d.* per day. One of the members of the Club caught last season here 1400 brace of trout; there are about three miles of river belonging to the Club. Adjoining and immediately below the Kilnsey water is another Angling Association, the Grassington Anglers Club, 30*s.* per annum, and strangers 2*s.* 6*d.* per day. The trout in this preserve are large and numerous. Willis of Skipton has a good supply of flies suitable both for the Wharfe, and

THE AIRE (Trout), Yorkshire.—This river is preserved from Gayrave to Carlton Bridge, about four miles by the Craven Angling Club; entrance 3*l*; sub. 2*l.* per annum; 25 members only, who however are permitted to bring a friend. Skipton is the best station on the Club ground.

At MALHAM TARN, a sheet of water belonging to Mr. Charles Morrison, the trout are very fine, running from 1lb. to 8lbs. nothing under 1lb. being allowed to be taken. The perch were formerly very fine, but have increased so much latterly that they have fallen off in size. Malham is reached by fly from the Belbusk station on the North-Western Railway six miles. Leave is difficult to obtain.

THE URE or YORE, in the North Riding of Yorkshire, Aysgarth.— Comfortable inn at Cross Flats, one mile and a half from Aysgarth Force. Fine scenery and a fly-fishing, conversable landlord. Route: rail to Richmond, thence ten miles to Aysgarth; or to Leyburn, thence eight miles.

THE YORE AND THE COVER (Trout), East Wilton.—Leave can be obtained from the landlord of the Blue Lion, East Wilton, three miles from the Leyburn station of the Bedale branch line. Also in the North Riding, Borrowbridge, on the line near the Tebay station, on the Lancaster and Carlisle Railway. A comfortable inn and fine scenery, with landlord as before.

THE DRIFFIELD.—The Driffield is fished by a club, and an occasional day may be given by a member to a friend; but the club is difficult to get into. Trout very fine.

Many of the Yorkshire rivers are ruined by mines and mills, and many others are strictly preserved. Few worth going to remain open.

THE WYE (Trout and Grayling), Bakewell, Derbyshire.—Very good trout and grayling fishing, with excellent accommodation, can be had by stopping at the Rutland Arms, Mr Greaves's. The tariff is reasonable, and the sport good; but very fine and good fishing is required to make a good basket. Anglers staying at the Rutland Arms have permission to fish from Bakewell to Haddon Hall, a distance of six miles by the river side, but two only by the road ; by remaining there more than a week they can also obtain permission to fish in the private parts of the Wye. Not far from Bakewell is Rowsley, where, by staying at the Peacock, the angler enjoys similar privileges. All flies can be had of the keepers. A portion of the Derwent can also be got at. By going to the inn at Ashford above Bakewell, we believe good fishing can also be obtained. The Derbyshire fish do not usually run large, seldom exceeding an *honest* pound, though they have been taken up to two.

THE DOVE (Trout and Grayling).—By stopping at the Izaak Walton Hotel, at Ilam, near Ashbourne, the angler may get leave to fish from Jesse Watts Russel, Esq., in three or four miles of the beautiful Dove, where he will find a keeper and all necessaries. The routes to all three of the above places are almost similar, by North-Western line, *viâ* Derby, and there are branch lines to Rowsley and Ashbourne. The scenery needs no comment here.

THE TEME (Trout and Grayling), Worcester.—Seven miles strictly preserved. Tickets, 15s. the season, or 2s. 6d. per week. The water is three miles from Worcester. Anglers are not restricted to the fly. Salmon are occasionally taken in the water—one or two having been already killed this season (1858). Tickets and information of any kind to be had on application to Mr Fredk. Allies, fishing-tackle maker, South Parade, Worcester. Route: Oxford, Worcestester, and Wolverhampton Railway, about four hours from London.

THE LUGG (Trout and Grayling), Herefordshire.—At Leominster, six miles, well preserved. By season, week, or day ticket. Close to the Leominster station at one end, and to Ford's Bridge at the other, on the Shrewsbury and Hereford line. Good accommodation at Leominster at the Oak Inn, where day tickets, price 2s., may be had.

THE COLNE (Trout), Fairford, Gloucestershire.—Three miles and a half of water. Good trout from three-quarters of a pound up to three pounds weight. Season from the 1st of April. Season tickets 2l., day tickets 2s. 6d. (not transferable), to be had of Mr Ferris, Bull Inn, Fairford. Route: Great Western Railway to Farringdon-road station by the 10 a.m. train from Farringdon. A coach from Farringdon-road to Fairford meets that train. Accommodation good, at commercial hotel charges. Mr Ferris will answer all queries. J. Ogden, tackle maker, Cheltenham, dresses a good fly for the last two rivers.

THE EXE, THE AXE, AND COLY (Trout), Devon.—Most of these rivers may be fished without difficulty, either by leave or by staying at the various inns. On the Coly the angler must take a day ticket, to be had at Colyton, there being an association to protect the fishing there. To fish the Exe he had better go to the Exe Bridge Inn, near Dulverton. At Collumpton he can fish the Culm. At Axminster or Tytherleigh Inn he can fish the beautiful Axe, which is open to all from Tytherleigh to the sea, save a field or two, where leave can easily be got. For some distance above it is preserved, but leave may be obtained; or he can go on up to Crewkerne, where he can obtain a season ticket, 1l. 1s. (or a week or day ditto). There is a tackle maker who supplies flies at Axminster. The Yarty is a nice stream, strictly preserved; but leave is procurable. The Otter is another nice river, where it used to be necessary to get leave of Lady Rolle; but tickets are now to be had at Finny Bridge, 2s. 6d. per day. Ottery St. Mary's is a good point to fish from. The Teign is a pretty river, but a good deal poached; Bridford, perhaps, would be the best point to stay at, as it is some few miles from Exeter. The best trout the angler will find to be in the Otter, the Coly, Axe and Exe. In most of the other rivers, though the trout abound, they are mere skimpings. The angler contemplating a tour among the Devonshire streams had better go to Exeter, and pause there while he supplies himself with the necessary flies, and any information he may need, at the tackle makers' there. Or he will find Lyme Regis, on the coast, a good central point, whence many of these rivers can be reached, and where he will get lodging, &c., reasonable. The best way to get there would be by rail (South-Western or Great Western) to Dorchester, and on by coach. There is also a good trout stream at Lynmouth, North Devon, which can be got at by stopping at Jones's Lyndale Hotel. The scenery is very fine, and there are other attractions to tourists and sportsmen, the celebrated red deer cover of Brendon being adjacent.

SLAPTON LEA (Pike, Perch, and Rudd), near Dartmouth, Devon.—A fine lake, with plenty of pike, perch and rudd, which can be fished by persons frequenting the Sands Hotel, kept by Mr. Pollard. The charge for a punt and man is 3s. 6d. per day. The lake is only divided from the sea by the highway and a narrow beach, so the angler may add to his amusement that of sea-bathing, a combination not to be met with every day. Route: Great Western Railway to Totness, thence by steamer to Dartmouth, through some six or seven miles of magnificent scenery, and on by fly to Slapton Lea; or he may go direct by fly from Totness to Slapton Lea, about eighteen miles.

THE TAW AND THE TORRIDGE (Salmon, Trout, and Perch), Great Torrington, North Devon.—The Taw is a capital river. Terms: season tickets for salmon, 2l. 2s.; day tickets, 5s.; for trout and perch, 1l. 1s. and 2s. 6d. The perch are very fine, and a salmon may often be picked up, sometimes two or three in a week, and the peel fishing is very good. For information, flies, tickets, &c., apply to Mr J. D. Bastard, fishing-tackle maker, Great Torrington, who can also give any information to other rivers in North Devon. The minnow is a good deal used here. The Torridge is fished by an association, limited to twenty, the subscription 1l. 1s. per annum. The season is from the 1st of March to the 1st of *August.* There is a good stretch and variety of water. Mr Bastard will supply any further information, flies, &c. The scenery is fine, and lodging and accommodation cheap. Route: Great Western Railway and North Devon.

The Tone (Trout, Roach, &c.), Taunton, Somersetshire.—Tolerable fishing can be obtained at Taunton by applying to Mr W. Clay, fishing-tackle maker, Parade, Taunton, who will answer all inquiries. There are several other rivers and streams within easy distance of Taunton, which is not a bad locality for an angler to set up his tent for a week or a month. Great Western Railway.

The Avon (Trout, Grayling, and Pike), Fordingbridge, Hants.—By stopping at Mr Stewart's, the Star Inn, Fordingbridge, the angler may have very good fishing in two miles of the Avon, and also in other waters, where the fishing is admirable. No charge for fishing. The accommodation excellent and reasonable. The angler will hardly regret a visit to this pleasant locality. There is a tackle maker in the town where all flies can be had; or he can get them *en route* at Salisbury. Route: by Great Western or South Western rail to Salisbury.

The Stour (Pike and Perch), near Christchurch or Bournemouth. —2s. 6d. for a day ticket, or 2l. 2s. per season; 2s. 6d. a day for man and boats; 1s. for baits. South-Western rail to Ringwood, and on to Christchurch. The perch are said to run heavy, and the pike fishing is tolerable. The King's Arms, Newlyns, is convenient.

The Itchin (Trout, Grayling, Jack, Perch, &c.), Bishopstoke.—Four miles of water; twelve subscribers at 5l. each. Trout and grayling occasionally large, three or four pounds weight, and pike also fine. Apply to Mr Richard Ridgely, Fleming Arms, Swathling, near Southampton. Water about a mile from the Bishopstoke station of the South-Western Railway.

The Itchin (Trout), Winchester, Hants.—A large extent of water, well stocked and preserved. Season ticket. Number of subscribers limited. Apply to H. Pottle, fishing-tackle maker, Winchester. South Western Railway.

The Itchin (Trout and Grayling), Otterbourne, Hants.—By stopping at the little inn at Otterbourne, near Twyford. Rail to Winchester. Flies for the Itching at Pottle's, Winchester.

The Test (Trout and Grayling).—There is a portion of the Test fished by a club at Stockbridge, and sometimes a day may be got through a friend; by staying at the White Horse at Romsey, too, a portion of it is fishable, and a day possibly may be got at Broadlands and on other waters.

The Nen (Pike, Bream, and Chub), Northampton.—A very good river for general fishing, running from Northampton to Peterborough. The river near Northampton is leased to an angling society. Subscription 1*l.* 1*s.*

The Yare (Bream and Roach) Norwich.—Free fishing from boat 2*s.* per day. Sport excellent. July and August best months. Living at Norwich cheap. There is a good angling society at Norwich for the protection of the fish. Route : Eastern Counties Railway.

The Darent (Trout), Farningham, Kent.—Good trout fishing in the Darent by stopping at the Lion, Farningham. April and May, before the fish are too much fished over, will be found the most favourable months here. The trout are of good size. Route : North Kent line to Dartford.

The Wandle (Trout), Surrey.—The Wandle is generally very strictly preserved, and without an acquaintance with some of the proprietors or holders it is difficult to obtain leave even for a day. There are, however, two pieces of water, though of rather limited extent, which are open, and where any strangers can fish. They are of course much whipped; but still, if the angler be an adept, he may pick up a brace or two of nice fish any favourable evening in May. Beddington Corner is the largest extent of water; but Hack-bridge, which is about a mile further up the stream, is best supplied with fish. The flies are of the very smallest and most diminutive species, and the finest fishing is generally required to do any good at these much-fished localities. A fine fish or two may often be got by fishing late, after the usual frequenters of the river have done. There is a peculiarity in the Wandle somewhat unusual. No matter how bright and hot the day, or how clear and low the water, trout will rise when they would not upon any other stream. The author once remembers taking four and a half brace of fine trout, when the day was so hot that he narrowly escaped a *coup de soleil.* The fishing is of little consequence below Merton. Any London tackle maker will supply the flies.

The Colne (Trout, Perch, Pike, Roach, &c.), Uxbridge.—Barrat's Water, a very fine piece of water. The season ticket to fish is 4*l.* 4*s.* ; or it can be fished by day ticket for trout, 5*s.* ; bottom fishing, 3*s.* The trout are very fine, being frequently taken three or four pounds each; but they are shy, from much fishing, and require an artist to secure them. A good many are taken with the minnow. There is a room constructed on all the weirs for the convenience of anglers, where they can dine, or leave their tackle, &c. The bottom fishing is very good, thirty or forty pounds of fine roach and dace being often taken, while chub, perch, and jack are also plentiful. There is a fishing-tackle maker at Uxbridge, whose flies may be found desirable. Route to Uxbridge by Great Western Railway.

There are other waters on the Colne, where fishing may be had by subscription or otherwise below this ; but the next water is the Thorney Broad water, near West Drayton. The Thorney Broad water may be fished by subscription, 10s. 6d. per season, or by a day ticket which costs 1s., which can be got at the water. There are a few fine trout on the water, *which require catching*, and there might be more if the water had a fair chance. There are also jack, perch, and bream, with some good roach holes, where the roach run heavy. The fly-fishing for dace, which are large here, is also good. Route to West Drayton by Great Western Railway. There are other parts of the Colne where leave *may* be obtained, as at Mercer's Mill, at West Drayton, and Uxbridge also ; but it is uncertain. At Rickmansworth, Watford, and down to Denham, the trout fishing is very good. At Rickmansworth there is a club, the subscription to which is either three or five guineas per annum ; and about midway between Watford and St. Alban's (Mr Alfred Gould, of Great Marylebone-street), has an excellent piece of water, about a mile and a half, well stocked with good trout. He lets the water, and this season it is taken by two gentlemen ; rent sixty guineas, Mr Gould finding keepers, &c. Below Rickmansworth there is good bottom fishing in the Coppermill stream, which is rented by a fishing society at Clerkenwell. On the Chess, a tributary of the Colne, at Chenies and Charlewood, the trout are very abundant, and thirty or forty brace of good fish, of about a pound or over, might be taken in a day. It is, however, strictly preserved, though possibly a *gentleman*, by going properly to work, might get leave from some of the proprietors, and it is well worth the trial.

THE KENNET (Trout and Pike), Hungerford, Berks.—Good trout fishing, by season ticket, 2l. 2s.; or by month, week, or day tickets, 1l. 1s., 10s. 6d., and 2s. 6d. respectively. J. Platt, Esq., is the secretary ; but any of the inns will supply the angler with a ticket. The trout are fine and plentiful. Flies of any of the London tackle makers. There are also pike in some parts of the waters—in fact, they have rather increased of late years. Season, from the 1st of July to the end of Agust ; but the trout are not in good condition before May, and hardly then. Route : Great Western Railway to Hungerford.

THE WICK (Trout and Bottom Fishing).—At High Wycombe, Bucks, there is a very beautiful little trout stream, where the trout are exceedingly fine—two, three, and four pounds, or even up to six or seven pounds, being not unfrequently caught, and of very fine flavour. The greater part of the fishing belongs to Sir G. Dashwood, who gives the right to his tenants, the millers on the banks; and, with one or two *liberal exceptions*, there is a very hoggish spirit amongst these men, who will not permit a rod of any kind on their water, not fishing themselves. They will neither give nor let, but draw the water down every year, and grope the trout out of the mud and knock them on the head. The entire water is but of short extent, however, not *above* three miles—for immediately below the town there is a paper mill, and paper mills occur at intervals for the entire remaining course of the river till it joins the Thames; and, owing to the shameful and unnecessary casting of the refuse bleach into the waters, nine miles of one of the most beautiful and prolific trout streams in England is utterly destroyed.* However, there are two pieces of the river open, about half a mile, perhaps, in all—one on the London road, and one on the Oxford road. The Oxford bit is the best; but they are hardly worth going to fish, and I only mention them should the angler be there with a spare half-hour on his hands. There is, besides this, an open bit, called The Dyke, which is a branch of the river, and runs through Lord Carrington's grounds, that contains fine jack and perch, with tench and large carp, and an abundance of very fine roach. An application to Lord Carrington's steward will easily obtain permission to the *whole* extent of the water, if the family be not there, which it seldom is. The author has passed many pleasant afternoons on the grassy banks and under the waving trees of this pleasant piece of water. The only millers a stranger would have a chance of obtaining a day's trout fishing from would be Mr Thurlow or Mr Lane; and, as their water is very limited, it would be most uncertain there. The latter gentleman has some good jack in his water. Sir G. Dashwood sometimes gives leave to fish in his park at West Wycombe, and there are jack, perch, &c. and some trout. The flies are rather local: peacock herl bodies, red and black hackles, with either ruddy brown speckled rump feather of a game hen or the wing feather of the jay; red spinner, moths for evening, &c. Route: Great Western Railway, branch line.

THE WINDRUSH, Witney, Oxfordshire.—There is, or *was* (for it is much poached) fine trout fishing here. The fish are equally fine and large with the High Wycombe fish. They are not plentiful, however,

---

* The law provides a remedy for this most needless sacrifice—needless, because there are many streams (as the Chess, for example), not twenty miles from Wycombe, where there are paper mills and also plenty of trout. It would be easy, and would pay the manufacturer, to construct tanks.

though they might be if protected. There is little difficulty in getting permission of some of the proprietors below Witney, but it would hardly be worth going there on the chance. The Mayfly comes very full on the river, and the author once caught some very fine fish just previous to its appearance with one of the flies named above (peacock body, blue hackle, and jay wing). The minnow, however, is more used there than the fly. The river abounds also with crayfish.

THE THAMES.

Few rivers have been the subject of so much writing as the Thames, and few are so capable of bearing its admirers through, whether we consider the varied beauty of its scenery, or the number, variety, and excellence of its fishes. There are few fish of their species equal in point of excellence, either for the table or for sport, to a Thames trout (the days of its salmon are, we fear, departed, never to return), a Thames jack, perch, flounder, &c., &c., to say nothing of the punch and brown bread and butter, and capital sport, which usually accompany the taking of that little fried thingumy known as whitebait, which forms, with its cayenne, lemon, and &c.'s, so very potent an excuse for drinking and paying exorbitantly for it. Judging of the whitebait by this standard, it should be the most delicious of modern absurdities.* But, as fishing, not eating, is our object, we will at once proceed to it.

The conservancy of the Thames has, until lately, been vested in the Lord Mayor and Corporation of London. It is now under the charge of a separate Government Board. The fishing, as far as Staines, has been and is protected by the Thames Angling Preservation Society—a society well worth the support of every angler who takes pride and pleasure in *his* river, for few rivers are so entirely free to the angler as the Thames. The first preserve on the Thames is the Richmond preserve, where there are plenty of roach, dace, and barbel. Below Richmond and down to Isleworth there is very good whipping for dace in the season. There are plenty of puntsmen at Richmond, and the usual charge is 5s. per day for a man and punt. Although the tide often interrupts sport for an hour or two, when flowing up it gives the angler this advantage over localities situated above the tide: the constant change of water keeps the fish feeding, which cannot be the case far above Teddington Lock, where the tide in a great measure ceases, and where, until towards evening, in very hot weather, the fish feed scarcely at all by day for many days and even weeks together. Thirty, forty, and even fifty pounds weight of roach,

---

* Query: what would a gourmand think if he were set down to a plain dish of fried whitebait and potatoes, with simple ale for a potable?

dace, and barbel may often be taken in a day. Good sport may be had at times, when the water is high, off the banks here.

The next preserve is the Twickenham preserve, a nice little preserve, with a deep hole, in which are barbel and some bream. There is also good roach and dace fishing.

Teddington is not a preserve; but there is good fishing there nevertheless for good barbel and dace, and the weir often gives up a good trout or two.

Above the lock is the new preserve, made only last year—a longish piece of water, containing good harbours for pike, perch, and chub; and as the Angling Preservation Society have been at great expense in staking and sinking numerous punts, iron waggons, and all sorts of things in the deep, it is hoped and expected that this will be, next year, the best deep on the river. In high water there is always good roach and barbel fishing here, and of course now it will be much improved.

Teddington or Kingston will be the punt station for this preserve.

Kingston comes next, and here the barbel fishing is at times good, and a few pike are taken, but the preserve is short and inconsiderable.

Thames Ditton comes next, and there was a time when this was a grand preserve, well stocked with all kinds of fish, particularly barbel and jack, and many a good trout. A trout or two is still taken on the shallows from here to Kingston, and sometimes a jack or so; but its glories have been largely shorn. At Hampton Court is a deep hole, opposite the embouchure of the Mole, called the Gallery Hole; it is not preserved, but holds a few pike, perch, and other fish, which come constantly from the Mole. From Hampton Court bridge to the weir is a preserve, where many good trout are taken, and occasionally barbel; but the destruction of the deep hole opposite the lock, which formed the principal harbour of the fish, a few years since, has told severely on the fishing. From the weir, the branch of the river on the Middlesex side is one continued preserve up to Hampton, and here jack, perch, chub, bream, and roach are plentiful, and *were*, a few years since, still more so. Here is Harvey's Ait, where a patient bank fisher can hire a stand and a seat at 1s. per diem. Opposite Hampton is a good shallow for trout, which are often taken of fine size there.

Sunbury is the next preserve, and the weir, with the long shallow below it, is famous for trout. The barbel fishing also is at times very good; but the river has been so altered by the dredging machines, &c. employed at the new lock, that we can hardly say at present what the prospect of sport may be—but, as many deep holes have been created, we should be inclined to think good.

Walton comes next. There are two preserves here, and a good variety of fish—jack, perch, chub, bream, barbel, and roach; but few trout. The bank fishing is tolerable.

Halliford has good fishing for barbel, jack, and perch; but it is not preserved.

Shipperton *was* in high repute, having three good preserves. A year or two ago some of the fishermen were detected netting the deeps. Still it holds good barbel, chub, roach, dace, perch, and jack; and the bank fishing is good.

Weybridge has a large and an excellent preserve, and very good trout fishing—perhaps as good as any under the charge of the Thames Preservation Society. There are also plenty of pike, perch, barbel, chub, roach, dace, and bream; and, as the Wey falls in here, it constantly feeds the preserve. The bank fishing is good.

Chertsey has a good preserve, and a weir; and the fishing for jack, perch, chub, and roach, is very good. There is also the Abbey river, in which is fair fishing.

At Laleham the trout, dace, and chub fishing is good.

Penton Hook has a fine and extensive preserve; and the fishing is similar in character to the last, but better.

Staines is the last station under the society's charge, and the preserve is good—containing large barbel, roach, and chub; and, towards the embouchure of the Colne, which runs in here, there are plenty of pike and perch. Indeed, the pike fishing generally is pretty good.

From this the Thames winds past Windsor, Datchet, Maidenhead, Cookham, Marlow, Médenham, Henley, Wargrave, Reading, Pangbourne, Streatley, Goring, Wallingford, Abingdon, and so on to Oxford—all of which are fishing stations. The best of them are Cookham, Marlow, Pangbourne, Streatley, and Wallingford. Marlow has a fine weir and good trout, pike, perch, chub, and roach fishing. At Streatley there is a capital association, subscription 1*l*. Wallingford has a fine deep pool, where large trout and jack disport themselves.

We subjoin a list of the inns and stations, to the landlord of any of which the angler will do well to write the day before if he wished to engage a punt:—

Richmond.—The Talbot and The King's Head.

Twickenham.—The King's Head; the Railway Hotel.

Teddington.—The Royal Oak; Kemp's.

Kingston.—The Sun; (at Hampton Wick) The Swan and The White Hart.

Ditton.—The Swan.

Hampton Court.—(Moulsey side) The Castle; (Hampton Court side) The Mitre and The Greyhound.

Hampton.—The Red Lion.

Walton.—The Duke's Head.

Halliford.—The Ship.

Shepperton.—The Anchor.
Weybridge.—The King's Arms, The Lincoln Arms, and The Crown.
Chertsey.—The Cricketers.
Laleham.—The Horse Shoes.
Penton Hook.—The Horse Shoes.
Staines.—The Swan.
Windsor.—Crown and Anchor, Three Tuns, Swan, and White Hart.
Datchet.—The Angel and Crown.
Maidenhead.—The Orkney Arms.
Cookham.—The Bell and Dragon, and The Ferry House.
Marlow.—The Anglers, and The Crown.
Medenham.—The Ship.
Henley.—The Angel; the Red Lion.
Wargrave.—The George and Dragon.
Reading.—The Railway Hotel.
Pangbourne.—The Elephant.
Streatley.—The Swan.
Goring.
Wallingford.—The George, and The Lamb.
Abingdon.—Crown and Thistle, and Lion.

In conclusion, we would offer the would-be Thames angler the possession of an invaluable wrinkle or two, which are the whole secret of the art, as regards the Thames. Fish as fine and as far off as you conveniently can. Do not kick up a row nor tumble into the water, nor fall asleep on a weir beam, nor drink too much bottled stout in hot weather; smoke as much as you like—it's a contemplative recreation, inclining to quiet, and moreover keeps the mouth shut. See that *all* your baits are not only well scoured, but as clear, clean, and brilliant as possible—there is more in this than people think for. Do not overdo your groundbaiting—a little of what is generally used would not only suffice, but would vastly improve your takes. Whenever you bait a pitch, bait it twenty-four hours previous to using it; and practise sedulously that amiable quality, patience. Beyond all this, as a sportsman and no pot-hunter, return to the water all under-sized fish, or fish which you do not require for some purpose; and *see* that this is done—do not leave it to the fishermen. Keep a civil tongue to all folk—and so mote ye prosper!

The charge for man and punt *above* Richmond is 7s. per day, and the man's dinner, or about the same price as good salmon and sea-trout fishing. Almost all the stations named can be reached either by or from stations on the South-Western or the Great Western Railways.

THE RIVER LEA.

This river is held in great repute by London anglers. It contains much the same fish as the Thames, though there may be perhaps more carp and tench and less barbel. Some of the waters are private; some rented by inns and clubs, where a subscription of some kind is necessary to enable the stranger to fish.

The first water is the White House, bottom fishing 1s. per day. Trolling and live-bait fishing is confined to subscribers, who pay 1l. per annum.

At Tottenham Mills, or Tyler's Water, the subscription is 1l. 1s. per annum for trolling, &c., 10s. 6d. bottom fishing without trolling, or 1s. per day without trolling.

Ford's Water.—Terms the same as the last water.

Bleak Hall, or Wicks's water, near Edmonton.—There is near three miles of water with good jack-fishing. Terms the same as before.

Chingford.—Digby's water; 26s. first year, 21s. afterwards. No day tickets or annual for bottom fishing *only*.

Ponder's End, two miles and a half, 10s. 6d. per annum. or 1s. per day.

The Ordnance fisheries, Enfield.—Swan and Pike Tavern, 1l. 1s., 10s. 6d., and 1s. as above; three miles well-stocked with all kinds of fish. A good water.

Waltham Abbey.—Permission obtained from the Ordnance, though some of the waters are let to the landlord of the King's Arms. Subscription 1l. 11s. 6d. No Sunday fishing. Four miles and a half excellent fishing.

Captain Sanders's Water.—Very good for the fly.

Broxbourne.—The Crown; subscription 1l. 1s., or 2l. 2s. with trout-fishing; day-ticket with trolling, 2s.; without, 1s. Very good.

Pages Water—1l. 1s. per annum.

The Rye House.—Five miles of water, with two weirs. The subscription is 2l. 2s. per annum each, to twenty-five members. The landlord can give permission to persons frequenting his house, for bottom fishing only. Sundays excepted. The Rye House is a very attractive place to stop at, and is much frequented.

For some distance above this the water is private, until we come to the Amwell Magna fishery.

The Amwell Magna fishery is the best of the subscription waters on the Lea. It is confined to twenty subscribers, at 4l. 4s. per annum each.

Above this the water is chiefly private, and the trout are more numerous than below. Indeed, the fishing is generally very good, but not easily to be obtained. We may, however, mention Hatfield Park, and Brocket Hall, where leave *may perhaps* (though it is by no means a certainty) be obtained. The Jonner belongs to the Marquis of Salisbury.

The Caller to Lord Palmerston. Hatfield and Welwyn on the Great Northern are the stations. The fishing is principally pike.

The Eastern Counties Railway will convey the angler to any of these stations, and he will generally meet with every attention, good accommodation, fair sport, and reasonable charges. He had better, however, take all necessary baits, &c., with him.

PONDS, PRESERVES, &c.

Amongst the various ponds, reservoirs, and other fisheries, we may briefly notice—

The Newington reservoir.—Good perch and roach, and a few jack. Leave obtained of the directors of New River Company, each of whom is allowed two tickets per annum. The use of a boat is only allowed when a director forms one of the party

The Kingsbury reservoir.—Mr Warner's, the Welsh Harp, near Kilburn-gate, on the Edgeware-road, where there is capital pike and perch fishing, at 1*l.* 1*s.* per annum. Day tickets for pike and perch, 2*s.* 6*d.*; for roach, 1*s.* Punts, live bait, and every other accommodation can be had on the spot.

The Ruislip reservoir, near the Pinner Station, North-Western Railway.—1*l.* 1*s.* per annum. Live bait found. A fine sheet of water, with a good variety of fish, including perch, pike, and roach. We believe a day ticket may be had, but are uncertain. It belongs to the Grand Junction Canal, and was to let lately; so an alteration may have taken place.

Frensham Ponds, near Farnham, Surrey.—South-Western Railway. Large numbers of perch; ten or twelve dozen in a day may be taken here, though mostly under half a pound. The man at the pond charges 1*s.* per day, with use of punt. It is a large sheet of water, near three miles round. Whilst fishing on it some three years since, we saw that rare bird the osprey, or fishing eagle, hovering over the lake; and ever and anon dashing down into the water, he bore away some victim in his grasp. N.B. Take provisions, &c.

Dagenham Breach, on the Essex marshes, contains a large stock of various sorts of fish—pike, perch, carp, tench, bream, rudd, roach, eels, &c. Subscription 1*l.* 1*s.* per annum, or 2*s.* per day.

The Hampstead and the Highgate ponds, which contain a few perch and carp, hardly need mentioning.

There are some ponds, too, both on Clapham and Wandsworth Common, which contain a few jack, perch, carp, and roach; are easily approachable.

There is a fine sheet of water in Wimbledon Park, which contains good pike, perch, and roach; and leave to fish which can be obtained by applying to the County Fire Office, or to Barber Beaumont, Esq., West Hill, Wimbledon Park.

There is also a good pond near Hanwell, containing pike, bream, and tench in large numbers. The man at the mill charges 1s. per day for permission.

Perch, pike, roach, and dace fishing can also be had on a small branch of the Colne, which runs into the Thames at Isleworth, by applying to the head man at the mills there, or by going to a little inn by the road-side, close to Whitton. Further on there is a subscription water at the snuff mills, halfway between Hounslow and Bedfont, where there is good jack, perch, and roach, and capital bream fishing. About half a mile beyond this, again, is a water rented by the landlord of a small public on the Bedfont road, named Daws, who gives permission to fish; and the jack fishing is very good in tolerably high water. Route: South-Western loop line.

In Richmond Park the Penn ponds contain numerous jack, with fine perch and very large carp; but the ponds are very weedy. Leave to be obtained of Col. Liddell, Deputy Ranger, 49, Cadogan-place, Sloane-street. A special permit is required to get the punt, which is not always obtainable. We have often taken from fifteen to twenty jack in a day there.

Home Park, Hampton Court.—Leave obtained at the Master of the Horse's office. There are three ponds and the long canal. The Cow-house pond once held very fine jack, and may still, but it is very weedy.

The Hampton Wick ponds contain many jack, but are so weedy as to be unfishable save in very high water. The long canal holds a few jack, fine perch, and very large carp. The Prince of Wales is ranger of Bushy Park, and leave is difficult to obtain; nor is it worth the trouble, as the best pond, the Diana, was not long since cleared out.

Virginia Water and the Great Lake in Windsor Park.—An order here is difficult to obtain, and never useable while the Royal family are at Windsor. An order may, however, *perhaps* be obtained through Col. F. H. Seymour, the Deputy Ranger, who lives at Holly Grove, Windsor Park. The Great Lake, at Cumberland Lodge, is the best place for fishing, and here the jack are numerous and large, and the perch fine and very abundant. Egham is the best *point* to go to for this piece of water. Should the fortunate holder of an order desire, however, to fish Virginia Water, he can go on to Sunningdale. On his order he will find the name of the keeper at Englefield-green, and he will do well to write to the keeper not only to make arrangements for meeting him (without a clear understanding on which he may easily lose half a day looking after him), but to let *him* know when the Royal family are away. Should he hook up a very handsome meerschaum pipe from the depths of the Great Lake, it belongs to the author. He must take *dace* and gudgeon with him; the keeper can only supply him with roach.

At Weston Turville, between Wendover and Aylesbury, near the Tring Station on the North-Western Railway, is a reservoir where there are very large pike occasionally, and an abundance of fine roach. Permission by subscription or day ticket. There is a comfortable little inn there, where the tickets are obtained.

At Shardloes, the seat of Squire Drake, near Amersham, about eight miles from High Wycombe, Bucks, is a very fine piece of water, abounding in jack. The owner sometimes grants permission.

The waters at Blenheim, near Oxford, are well-known. Immense jack and shoals of fine perch thickly tenant them, and leave may sometimes be got through the steward of the Duke of Marlborough; and if the angler is lucky enough to get a day there, and the day be favourable, it will be a red-letter day in his calendar.

There are numerous other ponds, reservoirs, &c., about London, which it would fill volumes to enumerate—at Stanmore, Middlesex; Chiselhurst, Kent; Gatton, Ryegate, Egham, and Godstone (subscription and day), all in Surrey. There are the canals, Surrey and Paddington; the New River; there is a pond at Garrat-lane, Wandsworth; another near Salt Hill (subscription and day). There is a little pond at Teddington; there is the Longford River, near Hampton; Mr Eley's ponds, near Hampton; the waterworks reservoirs at Hampton; the reservoirs at Hammersmith. In fact, their name is legion. In all of them more or less sport may be obtained.

There are about 800 rivers in England and Wales alone; and if we said 300,000 ponds, pits, reservoirs, and canals, we should be probably under the mark. We have endeavoured to point out a few of the best known to us; and if the angler succeeds in obtaining sport in any of them through our means, we shall have done our work satisfactorily.